Sherman

CARON LEE COHEN

WHERE'S THE FLY?

PICTURES BY **NANCY BARNET**

GREENWILLOW BOOKS, NEW YORK

Colored pencils were used for the full-color art.
The text type is Zapf Humanist 601 BT.
Text copyright © 1996 by Caron Lee Cohen
Illustrations copyright © 1996 by Nancy Barnet

Printed in Hong Kong by South China Printing Company (1988) Ltd.
First Edition   10 9 8 7 6 5 4 3 2 1

LIBRARY OF CONGRESS CATALOGING-IN-PUBLICATION DATA

Cohen, Caron Lee.
Where's the fly? / by Caron Lee Cohen ; pictures by Nancy Barnet.
    p.   cm.
Summary: Illustrations from increasingly distant perspectives locate a fly on a dog's nose in a flower bed by a house in a yard on a corner in a town near a bay on the earth.
ISBN 0-688-14044-0
[1. Visual perception—Fiction.]
I. Barnet, Nancy, ill.   II. Title.
PZ7.C65974Wh   1996   [E]—dc20
95-962   CIP   AC

For Max
and Bea Andler,
with love

—C. L. C.

For Alison

—N. B.

Where's the fly?

On the dog's nose.

Where's the dog?

In the flower bed.

Where's the flower bed?

Against the house.

Where's the house?

In the yard.

Where's the yard?

At the street corner.

Where's the street corner?

Across from the playground.

Where's the playground?

Behind the school.

Where's the school?

In the neighborhood.

Where's the neighborhood?

In the town.

Where's the town?

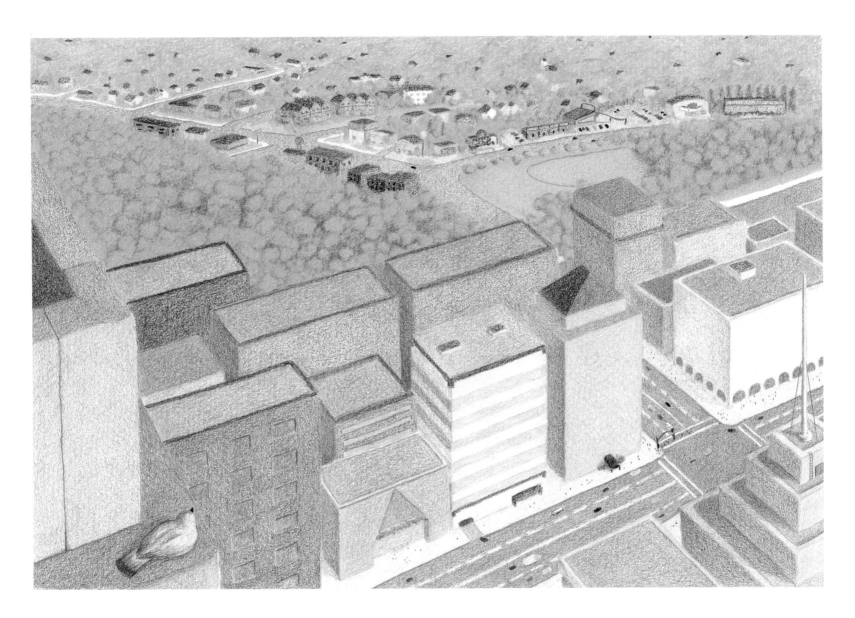

Outside the big city.

Where's the big city?

On the edge of the bay.

Where's the bay?

At the ocean.

Where's the ocean?

On the earth.

Where's the fly?

```
E        Cohen, Caron L.
C           Where's the fly?
```

GAYLORD F